A Christmas Angel Collection

12 Angels to Cut Out and Color

by Catherine Stock

WALKER AND COMPANY
NEW YORK

Chinaberry offers books and other treasures for the entire family.
For a catalog, please call 1-800-776-2242.

Published in the United States of America in 1996 by Walker
Publishing Company, Inc.

Published simultaneously in Canada by Thomas Allen & Son Canada,
Limited, Markham, Ontario

ISBN 0-8027-7499-7

Printed in the United States of America

2   4   6   8   10   9   7   5   3

For
Frances & Vere,
with special thanks to Susan

All you need is a pair of scissors (ask a grownup to help you with the scissors), a set of watercolor paints and brushes, felt-tip pens or colored pencils, and perhaps a little gold or silver paint to gild the tips of wings, halos, and other details.

Choose an angel and remove the page from the book. Color the angel before cutting. You can practice on a border to make sure that the color is not so dark or heavy that it blocks out the lines underneath. Decorate with gold and silver paint, stars, glitter, or anything else that catches your fancy. After the paint dries, turn the angel over and paint the other side. Cut out the angel along the outlines on the back and fold it up by bending the wings back and slipping tab A into slot B.

After the holidays, unfold the angels and pack them flat between cardboard to keep them safe and clean for another Christmas.

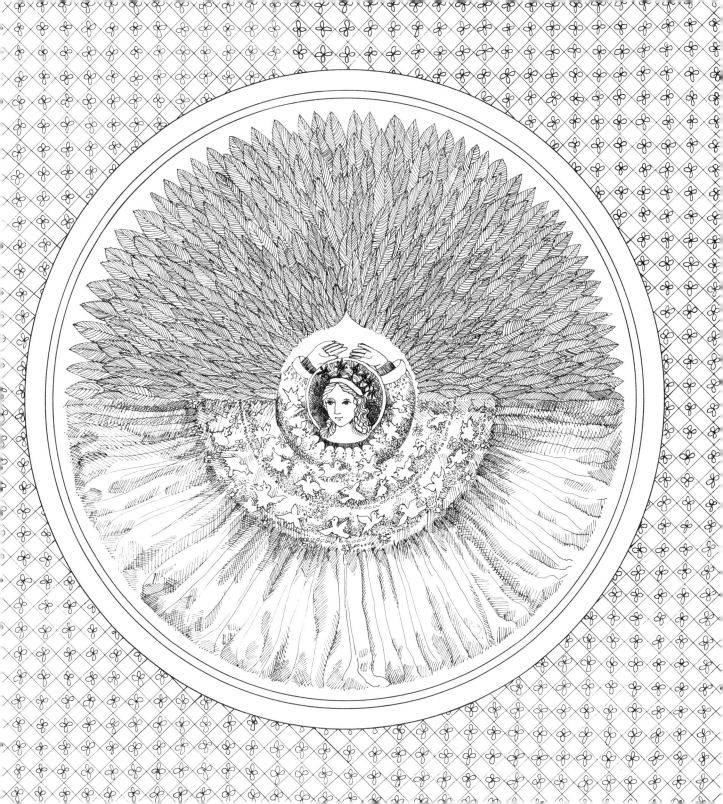

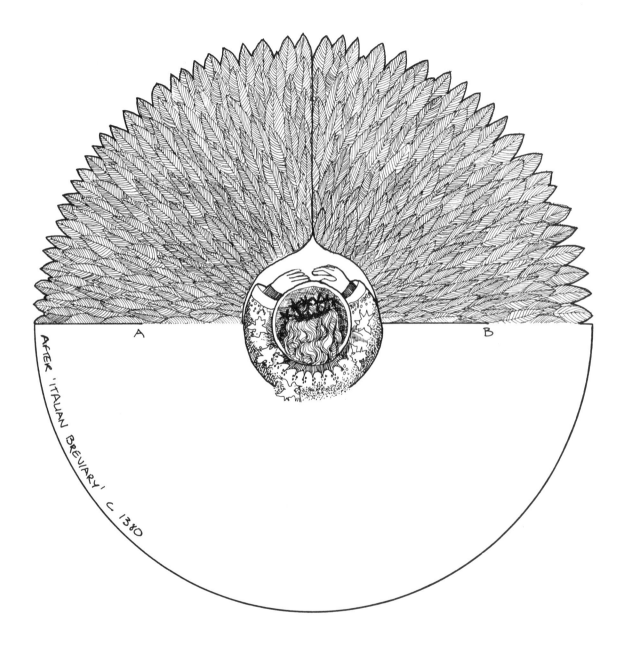

A

B

AFTER 'ITALIAN BREVIARY' C 1380

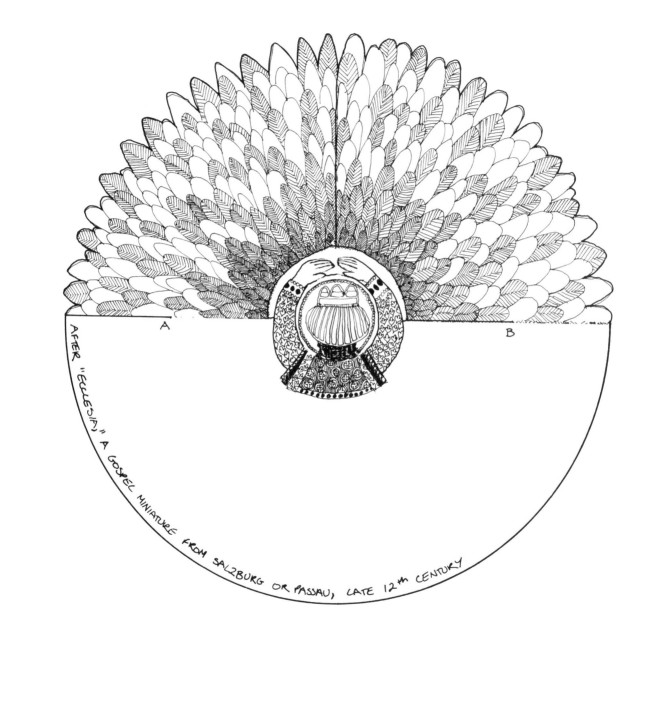

A   B

AFTER "ECCLESIA," A GOSPEL MINIATURE FROM SALZBURG OR PASSAU, LATE 12th CENTURY

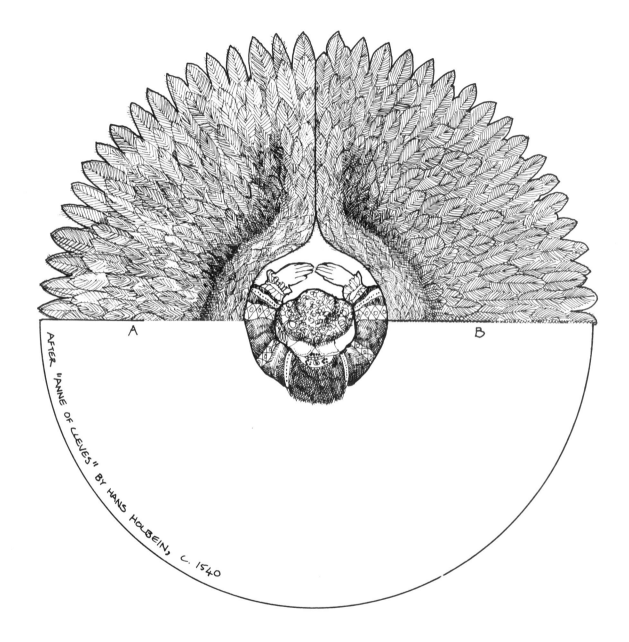

A

B

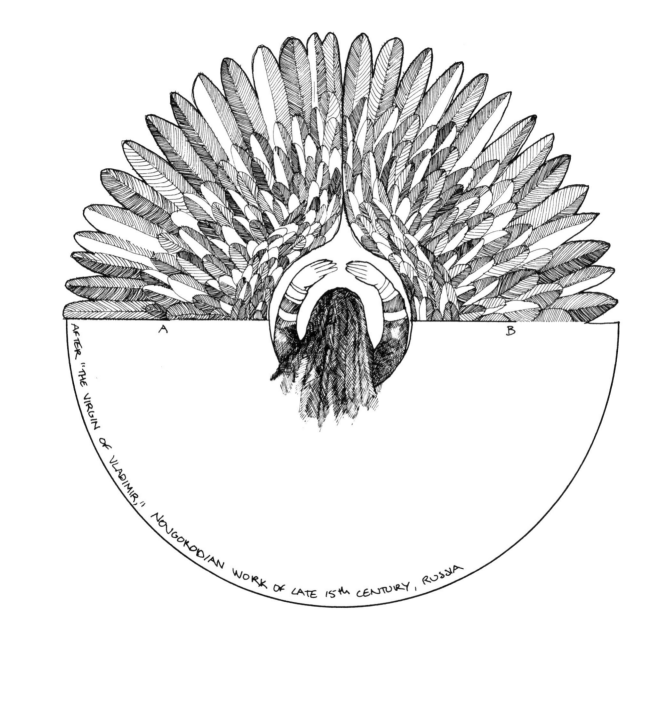

A

B

AFTER "THE VIRGIN OF VLADIMIR," NOVGORODIAN WORK OF LATE 15th CENTURY, RUSSIA

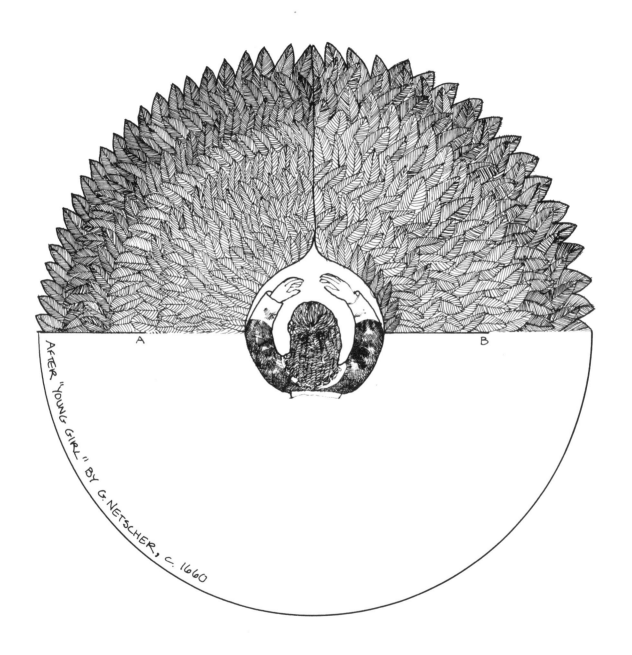

A

B

AFTER "YOUNG GIRL" BY G. NETSCHER, C. 1660

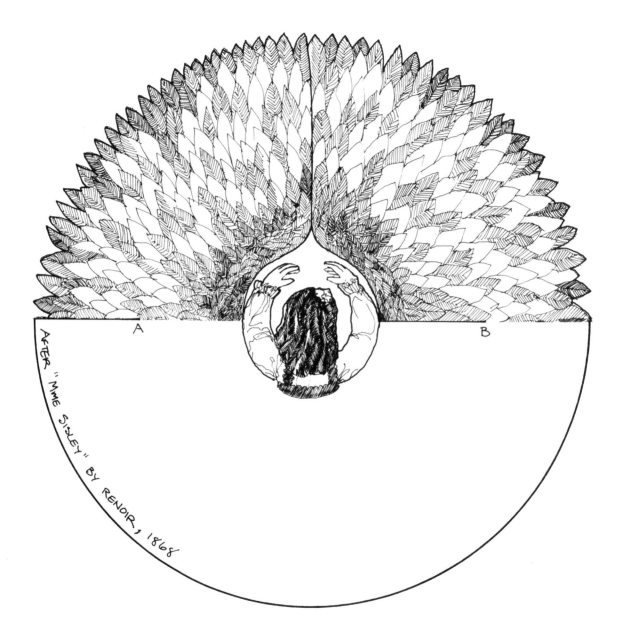

A

B

AFTER "MME SISLEY" BY RENOIR, 1868

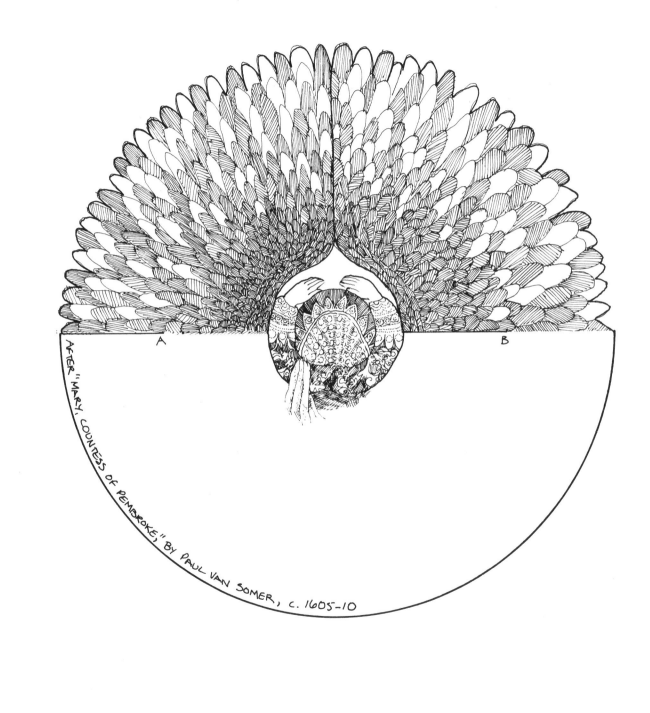

AFTER "MARY, COUNTESS OF PEMBROKE," BY PAUL VAN SOMER, C. 1605-10

A

B

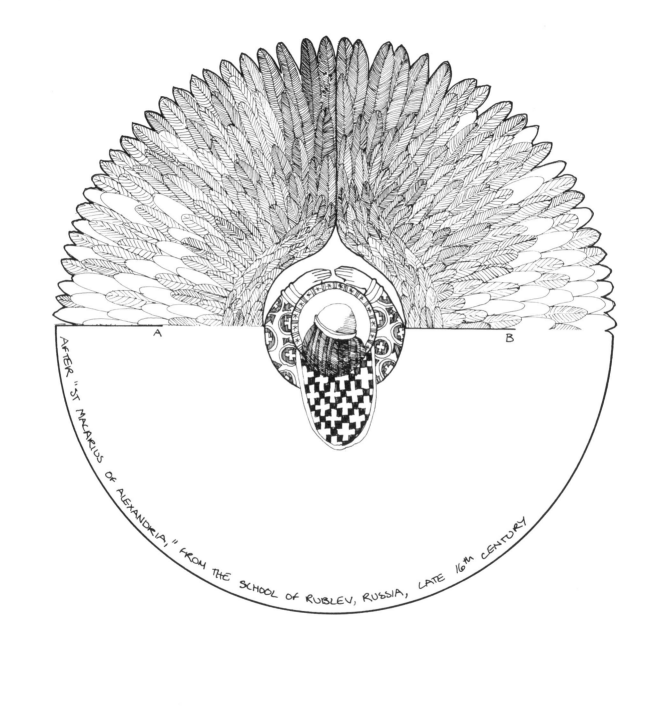

A   B

AFTER "ST. MACARIUS OF ALEXANDRIA," FROM THE SCHOOL OF RUBLEV, RUSSIA, LATE 16th CENTURY

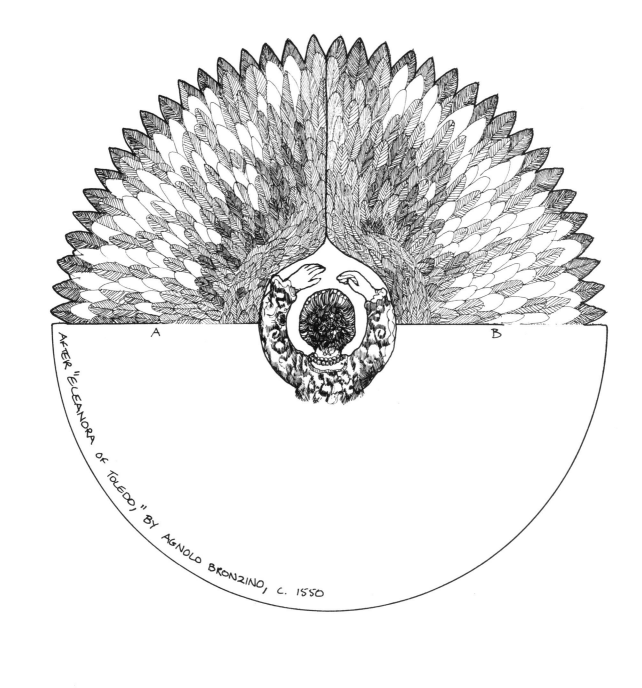

A   B

AFTER "ELEANORA OF TOLEDO," BY AGNOLO BRONZINO, C. 1550

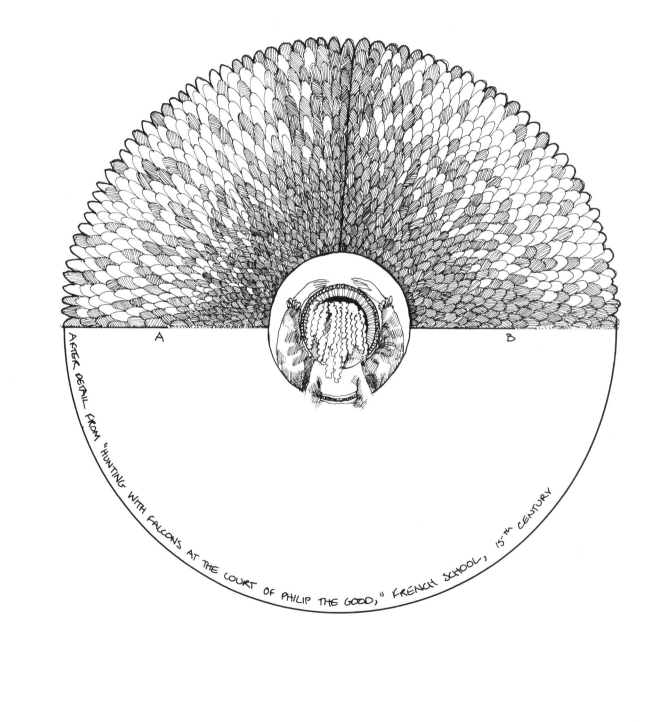

A

B

AFTER DETAIL FROM "HUNTING WITH FALCONS AT THE COURT OF PHILIP THE GOOD," FRENCH SCHOOL, 15ᵗʰ CENTURY

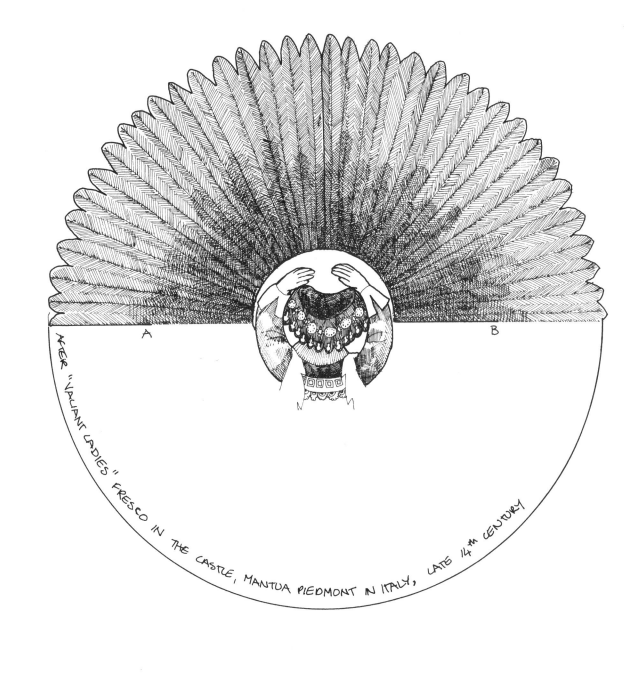

A

B

AFTER "VALIANT LADIES" FRESCO IN THE CASTLE, MANTUA PIEDMONT IN ITALY, LATE 14th CENTURY

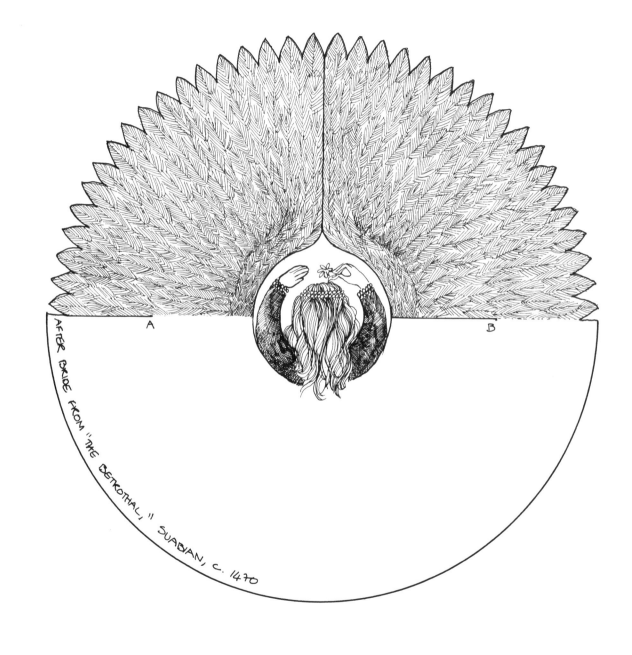

A

B

AFTER BRIDE FROM "THE BETROTHAL," SUABIAN, C. 1470